The Twelve Days of Christmas

Illustrated by Kathy Wilburn

Copyright © 1994 McClanahan Book Company, Inc. All rights reserved.
Printed in Hong Kong LCC: 94-75290. ISBN: 1-56293-495-3.
Published by McClanahan Book Company, Inc.,
23 West 26th Street, New York, NY 10010.

On the first day of Christmas
My true love gave to me
A partridge in a pear tree.

On the second day of Christmas
My true love gave to me
2 turtle doves
and a partridge in a pear tree.

On the third day of Christmas
My true love gave to me
3 french hens
2 turtle doves
and a partridge in a pear tree.

On the fourth day of Christmas
My true love gave to me
4 calling birds

3 french hens
2 turtle doves
and a partridge in a pear tree.

On the fifth day of Christmas
My true love gave to me
5 golden rings

4 calling birds
3 french hens
2 turtle doves
and a partridge in a pear tree.

On the sixth day of Christmas
My true love gave to me
6 geese a-laying
5 golden rings

4 calling birds
3 french hens
2 turtle doves
and a partridge in a pear tree.

On the seventh day of Christmas
My true love gave to me
7 swans a-swimming
6 geese a-laying
5 golden rings

4 calling birds
3 french hens
2 turtle doves
and a partridge in a pear tree.

On the eighth day of Christmas
My true love gave to me
8 maids a-milking
7 swans a-swimming
6 geese a-laying

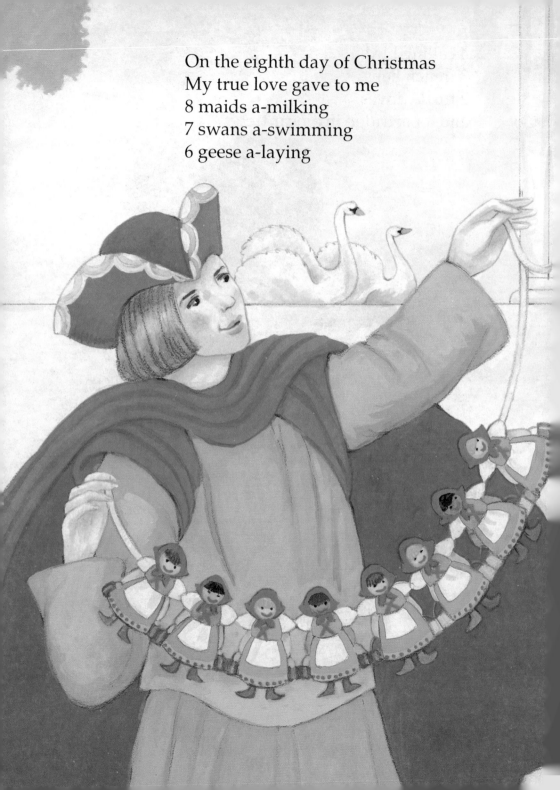

5 golden rings
4 calling birds
3 french hens
2 turtle doves
and a partridge in a pear tree.

On the ninth day of Christmas
My true love gave to me
9 pipers piping
8 maids a-milking
7 swans a-swimming
6 geese a-laying
5 golden rings
4 calling birds
3 french hens
2 turtle doves
and a partridge in a pear tree.

On the tenth day of Christmas
My true love gave to me
10 drummers drumming
9 pipers piping
8 maids a-milking
7 swans a-swimming

6 geese a-laying
5 golden rings
4 calling birds
3 french hens
2 turtle doves
and a partridge in a pear tree.

On the eleventh day of Christmas
My true love gave to me
11 lords a-leaping
10 drummers drumming
9 pipers piping
8 maids a-milking
7 swans a-swimming

6 geese a-laying
5 golden rings
4 calling birds
3 french hens
2 turtle doves
and a partridge in a pear tree.

On the twelfth day of Christmas
My true love gave to me
12 ladies dancing
11 lords a-leaping
10 drummers drumming
9 pipers piping
8 maids a-milking
7 swans a-swimming
6 geese a-laying
5 golden rings
4 calling birds
3 french hens
2 turtle doves
and a partridge in a pear tree!